THE NATIONAL POETRY SERIES

The National Poetry Series was established in 1978 to publish five collections of poetry annually through five participating publishers. The manuscripts are selected by five poets of national reputation. Publication is funded by the Copernicus Society of America, James A. Michener, Edward J. Piszek, the Lannan Foundation, and the Andrew W. Mellon Foundation.

1993 Competition Winners

Rafael Campo, *The Other Man Was Me: A Voyage to the New World*
Selected by Gloria Vando, published by Arte Publico Press

Martin Edmunds, *The High Road to Taos*
Selected by Donald Hall, published by
the University of Illinois Press

Karen Swenson, *The Landlady in Bangkok and Other Poems*
Selected by Maxine Kumin, published by Copper Canyon Press

Rachel Wetzsteon, *The Other Stars*
Selected by John Hollander, published by Viking Penguin

Kevin Young, *Most Way Home*
Selected by Lucille Clifton, published by William Morrow & Co.

THE OTHER STARS

Rachel Wetzsteon was born in New York City in 1967 and grew up there. After graduating from Stuyvesant High School, she received a B.A. from Yale University in 1989 and an M.A. from the Johns Hopkins Writing Seminars in 1990. She was writer-in-residence of the St. Albans School in Washington, D.C., during the year 1990–91 and is currently a graduate student in English at Columbia University, where she teaches composition. She has received an Ingram Merrill grant for 1994. Her poems have appeared in *The Kenyon Review*, *The New Republic*, *The Paris Review*, *Raritan*, *Salmagundi*, *The Southwest Review*, and other publications.

Penguin Books

Rachel Wetzsteon

*The
Other
Stars*

PENGUIN BOOKS
Published by the Penguin Group
Penguin Books USA Inc., 375 Hudson Street,
New York, New York 10014, U.S.A.
Penguin Books Ltd, 27 Wrights Lane,
London W8 5TZ, England
Penguin Books Australia Ltd, Ringwood,
Victoria, Australia
Penguin Books Canada Ltd, 10 Alcorn Avenue,
Toronto, Ontario, Canada M4V 3B2
Penguin Books (N.Z.) Ltd, 182–190 Wairau Road,
Auckland 10, New Zealand

Penguin Books Ltd, Registered Offices:
Harmondsworth, Middlesex, England

First published in Penguin Books 1994

10   9   8   7   6   5   4   3   2   1

Acknowledgment of first publication of some of the poems
in this book appears on page vii.

LIBRARY OF CONGRESS CATALOGING IN PUBLICATION DATA
Wetzsteon, Rachel.
   The other stars / Rachel Wetzsteon.
      p.   cm.
   ISBN 0 14 05. 8728 4
   I. Title.
PS3573.E945O87   1994
811'.54—dc20   93–38735

Printed in the United States of America
Set in Simoncini Garamond
Designed by Lucy Albanese

Acknowledgments

Cumberland Poetry Review: "Speech after a Spectacle"
The Kenyon Review: "Stage Directions for a Short Play"
The Paris Review: "Dissolving Views"; "Drinks in the
   Town Square"
Salmagundi: "Coming Back to the Cave"

Contents

I.

Urban Gallery   *3*

Terra Nova   *4*

Faraway Places   *8*

The Case of the Corpse   *9*

Falling in Love in Winter   *11*

When Love Takes Place   *12*

Blind Date   *13*

Flames and High Rains   *14*

Three Songs   *16*

From a Lecture on Loss   *21*

The Hunted   *22*

Garden Plots   *24*

Sestina for a Departure   *26*

Making Scenes   *28*

A Prayer to Hermes   *33*

A Prayer to St. Anthony   *34*

Bottom's Dream   *39*

Homecoming   *41*

II.

The Other Stars   *45*

III.

Question and Answer   *67*

Three Songs   *69*

Parables of Flight   *71*

Mirror Effects   *73*

Looking at Clouds   *75*

To a Passerby   *76*

Monologue for a Matron   *77*

Stage Directions for a Short Play   *79*

Venus Observed   *80*

Young Love   *81*

Drinks in the Town Square   *83*

Dinner at Le Caprice   *84*

Worms and Us   *86*

Dissolving Views   *88*

An Ode to Freedom   *90*

Speech After a Spectacle   *91*

Sea Change   *92*

Autumn Polemic   *94*

Taking to the Hills   *95*

Love's Passing   *96*

Coming Back to the Cave   *101*

I

Urban Gallery

When the wind invades the treetops
and the trees agree, shivering
take me, take me, when their
stealthy perfume drifts down to waft
among mortals, they come out in droves:
the boy whose bouncing keys speak a language
all their own, the novice who gets her tricks
from magazine molls (their haughtiness, swirl
of cleats), the gigolo with eyes lowered,
the better to judge his prey, the woman
whose hemlines rise as her age does,
the bad girl whose only remaining option
is to get worse: despite the string of cheats
and lukewarm reactions, she still has
the power to pound, the knack of
funneling her frustration into
the arrogant click of a heel . . .
at this armada of proud, unyielding soldiers
I have cast ferocious stones, holding forth
on barricaded gardens and souls' communion
until, heaving my bones from garret to gutter
I took to the street and saw it, too, was worthy.
Chasers out for a good time, flirters in
for a life's catch, strutters so skilled your
lurid designs burn holes, kill the cold
in the pavement, it does not matter
what fever you feed, so long as
you feed it freely; I hid my eyes
but sickness is catching; lovers, permit me entrance.

Terra Nova

I.

However quickly we hurry to the market
there is always a catch: the rake who stands
on the corner, hat hiding his true colors,
the golden boy who waits in a Renaissance window,
brocades and bedposts looming up
in the smoky recesses past him. There is
no entry here—unless I would give a good whistle
or bump into statuary—only
the sneaking suspicion of rooms just out of sight
and the shock of knowing their doors will always be bolted.

Although there is something to love
in this noonday bustle, I am more myself peering
into windows, looking for clues at a favorite's
favorite haunts, and letting slip, in turn,
now a hint, now a missing piece of the puzzle
to one who would know me; and
as you hand me produce to feel I am miles away,
finding no peace in the lands I visit,
tripping in a palazzo, and listening
with an ear forbidden to hear it
to that distant voice, that bolt of lightning.

II.

It is as if I am being chastened
by one to whom I spoke of historical
progression. Here are the same old symptoms:
the catch at the throat, the jellied extremities.
And here is the shamed examiner, holding

her strange new find to the light and thinking
moldy, but beautiful. Frayed, but I love it.
And here, worst proof of all of the never-
ending, harrowing course a fever
takes, is what I do to kill time:
panhandle until a coin with your picture
honors my cup; invent an ancestry;
bad-mouth my bedmate who drools like a spaniel;
listen for news of your whereabouts.

III.

If it were as simple as dentistry!
A tug at a tooth, or a cementing
of the hole, and no longer the ache
that runs in the nerve, the pang
in the darkest hour.

                          But the white coat
clings tightly to the patient, and if she
inspects herself it is only to crank
the key a notch tighter, while the doctor,
the renegade doctor, golfs or goes
yacht-hopping, caring no jot
about roots and diseases.

IV.

Suppose, by some high-handed show of
retribution, lightning struck nearby, chopping
a tree down, killing a child. I would

hear the news and gloat: for a blink's
span of violence there would have been no gap
between private slaughter and the world's travails.
Though no one would know it, the storm would have been
your presence writ huge, the spread-eagled
lifeless child my failure to foresee blows
and subsequent bruising. I'd make
the tragedy mine. Freaks of weather?
God's wrath? Wiring by ambitious newsmen?
I'd shake my head no, unnoticed.

What a height of monomania, that death should
deliver me; but what savage glee
to see one bloodbath mimic another,
quieter one, to deem an umber monolith
leveled by love. I will go there and breathe
the heady oxygen of a mission accomplished;
there is no longer any need to carve initials.

  V.

"There is no forgetting that one was"
never suffices. The wake of a glow,
the canned moment held to the light,
as now, open a world where the line
was cast and caught, but savagely
close the possibility of living healthily
here and now. What but a brooding
aftermath could follow the minutes of
halted breathing? How could I crown
the moment with anything but a ready-made
chain of roses? These suspended

bowls of kinship, these bubbles of hot air,
burst and swell at a pin's touch: you succumbed
willingly. Or, you were framed, distracted.
In this way the instant is never itself
but a succulent onion growing and growing
until the gritty truth of the matter is only
a nugget seen through veils, ornery
coverings I cut at only to weep over.
Soon even the knife and the tears will
disappear, the pith become fossil, and my hands
turn into animal claws, extended backward.

Faraway Places

Under a lamppost, faces lose their luster,
enter a world of accident and flaw.
Faraway places put me in a fluster.

Here in the street, a gallivanting cluster
of partygoers is obscenely raw.
Under a lamppost, faces lose their luster,

but when they scale a staircase they pass muster,
fill the bored spy below with newfound awe.
Faraway places put me in a fluster

because they let me play a mad adjuster,
trading my close-up chaos for their law.
Under a lamppost, faces lose their luster,

show me the naked truth behind the bluster,
make me confront his crimes, her painted maw.
Faraway places put me in a fluster,

and if an angel stooped I would not trust her;
how could a thing of beauty choose to thaw?
Under a lamppost, faces lose their luster.
Faraway places put me in a fluster.

The Case of the Corpse

It caught us in the middle of a picnic.
Having lugged our basket up a hill,
we'd opened it and spread its costly contents
onto a bright blue mat, and had enjoyed
approximations of festivity
when the corpse erupted on the scene.
It caught us in the middle of a picnic.

The body cast its shadow on the feast
gleaming before us; gaga over peaches,
poking rolls, praising tangerines, and
gulping down three kinds of intoxicants,
we had kept a wilting ball afloat
until, appearing weirdly out of nowhere,
the body cast its shadow on the feast.

Snow falling from its hollow cheeks and sockets
sobered us, stopping the discussion
dead in its tracks. Our subject had been weather,
its pleasantness that day, and its potential
never to rain again. We were beginning
a colloquy on sun when we discovered
snow falling from its hollow cheeks and sockets.

Older than the hills, but new to the setting,
the apparition shed a spotlight on
our feeble ploys to keep the picnic hopping.
Setting aside our strawberries, we spoke of
coves and troves we'd raided on the way up,
but past the bottled raptures, the specter lingered;
older than the hills, but new to the setting,

it stood between the hill and the horizon.
To solemnize the view was to invent
imaginary foes; to think our blanket
owed its profusion to the sky was wrong.
Where a world had been, a wall was rising;
where birds had sung, false notes took center stage.
It stood between the hill and the horizon.

What did it want, and where were its features going?
First its frosty head and then, limb by limb,
its body went, but not in the normal way
ghosts vanish. Looking down the slope for facts
to get the picnic back on its feet, we saw
its severed parts decaying in the forest.
What did it want, and where were its features going?

The phantom headed homeward for the kill,
though evidence of suicide deemed it dead.
Our fruit drew insects and our wine turned sour,
but closer to home were the strained smiles on our faces.
Apparently unwilling to accept
the carnage of the outing as sacrifice,
the phantom headed homeward for the kill.

Falling in Love in Winter

Falling in love in winter ought
to bring portents of spring, whether
the thought of a jet shooting up from earth,
nourishing as it falls, or glimpses
of vernal abundance elsewhere:
functioning sun, tall grass, running water.
But on walks by the edge of this frozen lake
it is nothing like that: what could be worse
than a flashy geyser, a vulgar display of
premature budding? A heart in trouble,
eyes that are used to scanning a room
are too much alive to deem a season dead
and only allow the sights of winter to be more
fully themselves: diligent flakes of
not-yet-snow help each other forward
in a stately pulsation of fugues
and bagatelles; the crunch of twigs
underfoot is no last gasp, but a crackle
giving evidence of a good long struggle;
the matted feathers of these sick birds,
evident signs of great decay, are only
false complaints to keep the rabble away—
what we, the fortunate ones, know and profit from
is that beyond the desolate chirps, beneath
the ravaged barks, everything present enjoys
subzero mayhem, a time of electric ice.

When Love Takes Place

When love takes place, places begin to take
stock of themselves, set their parts
in order. I am at school again, learning
to see from the ground up: here is
the ironwork table where we sat in
dawning awareness, here the dark hall
where you became a beaming face
among gargoyles, and here is our landing,
home to charged exchanges of weather
and subtext. Aliver still to the altering eye
are places I have not seen you but might:
this room is a swarming haven
of *quadratura* possibility—clinches,
parries that end otherwise, phrases
fit for me but no censor fill its
four walls. The garden waits for you as I do,
badly: there is something missing
from its oozy unwatched furrows and
air of being a stranger to change. All these
overbrimming places make "wish you were here"
a phrase for crooners; now there is only
"glad you were here, oh how you were here"
and "come again, stay forever." Such is your power
that after a kind word, landscape has a history,
buildings no small number of steps and corridors
to be spotted in, bowled over. Such is your threat:
that a snub or passing horror—are they only bricks
to you?—subtracts from the layout of land
what little moment it may have had;
it becomes worn down, lived in but none
too well, a catacomb for a liar, an architect's living.

Blind Date

Siren I have never seen,
only begetter of a brain where
synapses howl from crag to
crag, vast eons of daytime stretching
between them, popper of
flavorless gum, vision
in flames and taffeta, merry
wisecracker, dream in white and
would-be harpy, when you sprang,
gung-ho and tiara-first, out
of the mouth of the god who praised you,
was it you who committed atrocities
of hairspray then and there, or
are you only a slave
of the void who sees you
plucking at damaged harps, pecking
at heartstrings? When you two tango
down the runway, where will you put
your pitchfork? Is it good
to be young? When you simper
under balloons (black for appearances,
red for later, corruption's favorite
colors), what radiant halo
favors you, flees from me? What night
of no moon beckons? What
does he have in store for you? Reporter
to no one, aspiring tart and
unwilling virgin, can't you
pack up all your tricks and
bother another?

Flames and High Rains

Half awake, I ran through my dream: a fire
ravaged you, disfiguring all your features.
Why, when every third thought concerns you, would I
want to destroy you?

But tonight, traversing the rainy streets, I
see I orchestrated a fatal blaze to
reinstate you, just as each corner is a
hotbed of meaning,

each parked car a dripping reminder, not of
warmer motors elsewhere, but what inheres in
each parked car: a small, necessary part of
citywide efforts

to contain you. As I continue walking,
lashes wet (the only true way of seeing),
all my facile rides on a moral high-horse
are contradicted:

those for whom a decor becomes a credo
madden me; what depths are omitted! As for
dressing like a period, I admit its
frivolous charm, but

cannot take it seriously. So when a
city bears your personal imprint like a
formal envelope or a peopled snowcap,
how can I welcome

what I see, or testify to its beauty?
Easily, magnanimously. Tonight, all

roads converge in one, and as water fills these
welcoming highways,

even those who stifle their wonder feel its
elemental power. It is not fear that
makes the pavements shine, or the treetops send their
sweet perfumes downward,

but a joyful fervor to serve a despot
as benevolent as he is almighty.
Oh, high magistrate of the evening, make me
a mediator

for the souls who walk in your wake, unknowing,
for the fools who run from the rain and curse it.
Ruler over dark dissolution, let me
roam in your honor,

see you in the various shades of night, the
giddy competition between the streetlamps
and the rain, the sinister ambulance that
passes by, singing.

Three Songs

I.

Much has been said of the
amorist's tendency
to see the world as a
map of her mind.
If she repines for a
lone individual,
she fills her spare time with
loving mankind.

Teeming humanity
in all its wonders, though,
when I am love-stricken,
bores me to bits.
Better to hole myself
up in a mania,
rave in a ready-made
palace of fits.

Sociable nourishment
can't hold a candle to
salving a complex and
nursing an ache.
If a big breadline forms
outside my hermitage,
I bolt the windows and
let them eat cake.

Love, say the optimists,
makes the bewitched want to
run at the masses with

spread-eagled arms.
I do not rush out, but
hoard my obsession and
crabbily contemplate
burglar alarms.

It is their orderless,
intrusive otherness
that I must keep out—this
rival, that bore.
In the ongoing film
of my own martyrdom,
real life gets left on the
cutting room floor.

Otherwise it might swoop
down on the scenery
on wings of common sense
and call my bluff,
saying, "Your passion is
test-tube-begotten, your
much-vaunted lunacy
founded on fluff."

To which (to give myself
credit) I would respond
that it was sadly but
perfectly true.
If a delirium
cannot survive without
shutting the neighbors out,
what can I do?

Only continue to
come down with symptoms and
prune the green leaves of a
fruitful despair,
hating the plotters who
peer in my hothouse and
threaten to tell me that
nothing grows there.

    II.

What if I locked you in my chamber,
gave you a trauma to remember?
After the days of nonstop violence
and the long nights of grisly silence,
would your rock-hard, unwilling heart
say yes, though your lips said no?

What if I shredded all your papers,
treated your past as fuel for tapers?
Would your new name create new feelings,
or does identity have ceilings
past which a meddlesome invader
damnably cannot go?

What if I dug a moat around you,
questioned and kicked and gagged and bound you?
Solitude and interrogation
only make a capitulation
less sincere; your body may
say yes, but your mind says no.

What if I monitored your eating,
starved your resolve with prolonged beating?
You would possess a small figure
but your big spirit would get bigger.
Oh my triumphant captive, I have
dealt you an empty blow.

Roaring pain and induced affliction
cannot make inroads on conviction;
I check your cell each hour to find you
stubbornly loath to change your mind. You
wicked dissenter, your frail bones
say yes, but your heart says no.

What if I freed you from your shackles,
shoved you outdoors with jeers and cackles?
You would soon find the wide world staler
than your vivacious, loving jailer,
but if this hell is what you think
you want, you are free to go.

III.

How did you feel when you entered the church?
Left in the lurch!
What did they say when you brought back the ring?
Poor jilted thing!
Why did they laugh when they looked up its make?
It was a fake!

How did you spend your time out of town?
Tracking him down.

How did he look when you raided his room?
Pale as a groom.
What were the words the coroner used?
Vilely abused.

How many mourners can fill a hall?
Room for them all.
What are the songs the organist plays?
Dolorous lays.
What do you drop as you head for the bier?
Never a tear.

Have the embalmers earned their pay?
Pink hides the gray.
How does he look who did not survive?
Almost alive.
What does the crowd remark upon?
That he is gone!

How do you feel among these men?
Jilted again.
What do his benefactors sense?
Wasted expense!
Where is the world's most wanted dun?
Still on the run.

From a Lecture on Loss

In the textbook case, we see an infant purple-faced
over the brisk removal of a favorite doll.
For days she has engaged the thing in childish games
of many kinds: the age-old show of force, in which
toy collides with wall, only to be retrieved
and lovingly embraced; the twice-daily feedings;
if they are ever dirty, the cleaning of its features;
and happiest for us, the placing of the doll
next to her in bed, half smothered in eiderdowns.
In this way she has made a world where nothing harms
her prize possession, save her; steal it and see her crumble.

Flip to the appendix, gentlemen, and be brave.
Here is a case that never fails to separate
the squeamish from the strong: we gave a similar gift
to a similar child—in age, appearance, mental makeup—
but packaged it so well that she spent many hours
getting to know the box, and not the toy inside.
When she had loosened up the beribboned apparatus
enough to lift the lid, she squinted madly in,
at which point we removed it, and the outraged girl
fell to decorating the wall with smelly, obscene pictures
of what she never saw. Good fellows, what does this mean?

The Hunted

Where in God's name are you? This is not
the strangled cry of state-of-the-heart
indulgence, but a parched and overdue bid
for order; we may get up worshipping
the world that is never in the same place twice
and go to bed all the snugger for having done so,
but there is a rage, despite it all, for
hierarchical thinking. Knowledge of your
whereabouts provided a chart with one
circle of deep color, others moving concentrically
into whiteness. To be at all near the bull's-eye
was to make raids on the whole and the true;
to be anywhere else was to pale and kill time.
Your going further afield, if I had it in
writing, would only widen these circles:
it would be beet red in hotels abroad, a sort of
tissue pink at home; hammered gold where you
sipped at coffee, the yellow of trampled straw
in provinces you'd left hanging. But this suspension
lacks even the rudiments of an
itinerary! You could be blocks away,
miles and climates off; you could turn up
around the corner, or be off trying on
hats of the world: fezzes, bowlers, Tyrolean stunners.
Consequently, it is gallows time for rank,
and bands of angels have nothing to do.
The afternoon, having the potential to house you or
howl for you, hangs uneasily
in between. Do I love or despise it?
Knowing so little, I can do neither, but
only scour it, impatient for a sign.
The hungry are the world's best spies.

Alert to the point of mania, they dog a clue
to its every conclusion, standing disguised under
lampposts, with ears pricked near beloved addresses.
But human hounds need more than just trenchcoats
and cannot peer into blackness; the utter lack
of even a lead makes the profession tremble
and drop its steely machismo. Where in the world
are you? What can I do to staunch the slippery
landscape which may or may not be
concealing figures? Even the atelier is starting to
shut down; fantasies need hard facts to get them started,
vibrant dyes a firmly fixed, local color.
And therefore, renegade traveler, wherever you are,
send news: the air is alive with something, but it is
something evermore about to burn.

Garden Plots

Restless unruly spirit,
go if you must, but take note:
I will not stay behind to
sanctify your old haunts with
all the outpourings of the
usual useless vigil:
tears in the fading footprints,
blood on the barren altar.
Solitude breeds invention:
charting your every step and
getting there well before you,
I will become the Master
Architect of the Follies;
if forests on their own are
reminiscent of nothing
save other forests, if the
flower beds on your way are
lacking in evocation,
I will storm in and make the
necessary adjustments,
counting on garden plots to
keep me alive and with you.
Look at the bushes in the
park where you take a breather!
What, from a distance, seems a
uniform leafy cluster
spells out, on close inspection,
certain beloved initials.
What a surprise awaits your
eyes at your next location!
Innocent-looking flagstones
have been installed with buttons,

each of which activates a
different pair of statues
into an imitation
of one of our off-color,
passionate former poses.
How the hijinks continue!
Not a high-flying cloud is
without familiar features,
not a low oak without its
carven remonstrances and
clever nostalgic doodles.
Poor unsuspecting traveler.
Eagerly you embark on
journey upon long journey
only to find that you are
kept on a leash; in hopes of
clearing your head of all your
day-to-day drains and fetters
you flee from my embraces,
only to find that there are
no such things as vacations.

Sestina for a Departure

Now that you are about to be spirited
off to the gleaming portal of a world
where new aberrancies vie with old-world brick,
imagine, at the center of a whirlwind,
ready to plunge from her hidden, hovering branch
to your loud yard, an ever-present vulture

who watches you. She is a restless vulture
and does not wait for bodies to get their spirits
shaken out of them to abandon her branch;
as long as devils populate your world
she'll find their houses out and start a whirlwind
of terror simply by swooping from tree to brick

and—after the devils are done for—soaring from brick
to tree. For a greedy pack of earth-bound vultures
will offer you a different kind of whirlwind
which satiates the body but stunts the spirit;
to make a good impression in their world
you must agree to give up every branch

of learning for a leafy riverside branch
past whose shade a maid is waiting, thick as a brick.
But what if the smutty birdcalls of the world
win you over fair and square? The vulture
is short on common sense, but stubborn of spirit;
she paces her perch, imagining a whirlwind

of forcible seduction. But what if the whirlwind
grows too strong for the pendant, often-paced branch
to hold both the vulture's body and her spirit,
and you leave home to discover, spattered on bricks,

the horribly mangled body of a vulture
after her bloody collision with the world?

This would not be keeping watch on your world
but going from one overblown, deadly whirlwind
to another, changing the victim from vamp to vulture.
Better to roost, beak muzzled, on the branch,
watching you carve initials into brick
and remaining stiff of body, though sick in spirit.

If only the wayward spirit were solid as brick!
The vulture sits and wishes for a whirlwind
and the branch trembles slightly, high above the world.

Making Scenes

I.

Now that you are safely and briefly away,
let the garden flourish within its necessary
limits. Let its upkeep rest in the hands
of one for whom duty is not a burden
but a chance to cultivate greenery—from blighted
pockets let new grass spring; down from deserted
branches let foliage dangle. To let it run
to seed would be to show you a desolate sight
upon your return. But do not let the garden
get ahead of itself, turning out bud
after stubborn bud of flashy upstarts.
There is room for growth, not infusoria.
Save that extra push for a future arrival
and then let it thunder down in a shower of riches.

II.

The drumbeats banished, the bayonets
set aside or turned against their careless
bearer in a scuffle I do not understand
(all I know is that it works), I rest
from my warlike labors in the shield
of headrest and coverlet. But dismissal
only rouses the whole mad entourage
to more covert operations—through a
crosshatch of trees, a camouflaged hunter
stalks his prey; a bone-white stag is
bloodily downed; a violent tussle
breaks out over a twitching morsel of mouth-

watering meat. And the rising sun brings shame
and a prayer: give me the strength to be honestly awake.

III.

Each view is threefold. There is the topmost
layer of things unequivocally seen: the man
in loud pants, the forlorn sidewalk café, and the
ever-present pigeon who gnaws a wrapper.
There is, beneath these things but glaring
as black at a wedding, a list of what they are not:
not a loved one spotted, not the locus
of a tryst, not a rare, significant seabird.
And onto these two pictures clamps a troublesome
third, through whose distorting surface
birds are half swan, half sparrow, and slumming kings
and their well-dressed subjects eat lunch together.
This last layer, a patchwork of givens and
engineering, shakes the first two until nothing is solid.

IV.

Reduced to a pulpy stew of reflex and sentiment,
I purchase a book whose protagonist bears (I learn
from the backflap) your name. But you do not
enter right away: starting to read, I invest
the bustling extras with the colorless coating
of pupas in waiting, treat the setting and family history
as preparations for the feast ahead; all this
is entertaining warm-up, but warm-up still.

The season is then fixed, the time of day
and your pending arrival shown in a series of close-ups:
hedges poised between worlds, awnings erected.
I turn and burn the drama into the details
but when you show up, we have a problem:
the parents were great kidders; the protagonist is female.

     V.

No one sleeps. You too, in your chaste room,
are watching the stars that twinkle with love and hope.
Tonight, a secret is kept; if not tomorrow
then soon, I will reveal it on your lips
and conquer! and conquer! But secrets never wait
until dawn; I turn to the loyal lump beside me
and see his eyebrows lifted in rapt attention to
the words, his wet eyes very far off and brimming
with secrets of their own. Love is not lost
all at once, as in a door opening silently,
violently, onto a hotbed of sin, but in
smaller stages: the finicky care we lavish
on public faces, our private treachery over
the climax of an aria. No one sleeps tonight.

     VI.

It is best if he does not speak at all,
but if he does, let him speak no words in praise
of the place where we are spending a lean lunchtime—
a garden where I have sometimes seen you sitting—
nor list the winning qualities of the traitor

who grips his arm. Both would be gaudy streaks
of varnish on a painting signed and finished,
plaster forgeries where a copy existed
and sufficed. Your presence in the garden
takes the form of a fragile, unseen behemoth
swelling out the silences, clamming up
when somebody moves. If colloquy is murder,
what are we left with? Sentences that shatter;
lips sealed shut for fear the trees will shut up.

VII.

Guided to the summit of cold Mount Pazzo
by a sprite who hurried ahead of me,
stopping only to show me all the graves
of lovers who had perished along the way,
I gave the place the haughty look of one
whose long and bitter climb had not been wasted;
though the sprite had vanished, I would not rest
until he lingered on in marble men and
arable soil. But starting work on a statue,
I could not remember a thing about him,
seeing only my scarred, long-suffering feet,
my squinting eye and feverish complexion.
Worst of horrors, it was myself I'd sculpted.
Dime-store likenesses sprang up on the summit.

VIII.

This letter—having been smashed along with
the bottle, then pieced together by a careful

gathering of scraps along the shore—rests
in your hands. How would I have you read it?
In mounting frenzy and a gut urge to make
the capsized boat the very antithesis of a wreck,
paddling against the current to find it, and show
its sinking crew the pleasures of really getting wet?
In private torrents of tears which mourned
the fatal blunders of the inept captain,
commemorated the stoical, unlucky passengers
in floods closer to home? It is pretty to think
of both, but if you want to escape from the island
read on, the paper slightly damp with your tears.

A Prayer to Hermes

Hermes, messenger to the great,
I would solicit you to bring
a letter to a wayward friend,
a wayward friend to a waiting hearth.

But oh, my friend, there is no friend.
His heart surrenders God knows where
to snares not mine. It follows that
your holiness stoop to human tricks.

Half-man Hermes, patron of thieves,
send me a hood to hide my face,
help me to find the house in question,
then take the map so I cannot turn back.

Give me money to bribe the guards
but give me a gun in case they are large,
and as the door opens, ply me with weapons
stronger than steel, though harder to see.

Novice bandits welcome a hand,
but when my thieving steals me a heart
and the treasure stands to be counted,
fleet-footed Hermes, quit my sight.

A Prayer to St. Anthony
(Patron Saint of Lost Objects)

I was a shriveled woman with a blanket
    over my head,
pinning eternal wishes to your jam-packed
    wall of requests,
but it is for a favor that you have not
    handled as yet
that I genuflect to your splendid shrine in
    garrulous dread.

So many things are lost that your renown is
    not at all odd;
diligently you track down that prized ring, that
    filet of cod
someone set aside in a tizzy. But when
    I humbly nod
it is for no local misplaced thing, but a
    loved one abroad.

There will be no reveling when I find him
    under a chair,
or a pummeled head when I notice what has
    always been there,
hiding in a crack. He is of a mettle
    mobile as air,
hammering himself thin until he shimmers
    brightly elsewhere.

What should be the remedy for a friend left
    cruelly behind?
I could venture into the great outdoors and
    squint myself blind,
but I choose instead to address a well-known
    saint of your kind

with the panoply of protective measures
    I have in mind.

Visceral fears first: do not turn him into
    someone who lets
duchesses and doyennes ensnare him in their
    glamorous nets,
or surround him with an array of crude hail-
    fellow-well-mets
which erase his honor and raise the inter-
    national debts.

Keep him far from alleyway cabalas and
    hooligans' pranks,
let alone allowing him the false thrill of
    joining their ranks;
if you keep the coteries closed, the robbers
    robbing their banks
and not bruising bystanders, you will have my
    heartiest thanks.

Safety granted, take care that he is only
    physically lost,
and that after rarefied days of being
    gallery-tossed
and long nights of sipping expensive wines of
    infinite cost,
he is not unbearable when our paths have
    once again crossed.

Do not let the transcontinental splendors
    of the grand tour

bring him home a Euro-nostalgic phantom
     pallid and dour
who, when asked the meaning of life by someone
     unschooled or poor,
has the xenophobia in reverse to
     brand him a boor.

But (good saint) forbid him to undertake the
     alternate route,
coming back a resolute dandy in a
     tailor-made suit.
His new laugh and foreign expressions would be
     terribly cute,
but to catechize him would be to find him
     morally mute.

Lead him into lands with the skill to see the
     lead with the gold;
never catch him thinking an ornate square is
     good because old;
heads of brave dissenters have topped the poles where
     prints are now sold,
though time's wave has laundered the gutters where they
     bloodily rolled.

Slow his fevered pace to an easy lope—to
     rush is to miss
all the times when subtle attractions stir up
     gradual bliss;
hurried raids on pre-plotted landmarks make the
     slickest abyss
of the highest sphere, turn the sky into the
     Valley of Dis.

Give him strength of mind to observe the tinted
    and the blown glass
without the imprisoning, muffled cry of
    "This, too, will pass."
This is what a fool thinks when, finding
    pleasure in grass
and another's presence, he holds his tongue and
    saves it for Mass.

If he deems the gems of the old world golden
    but at the core
alien and best kept behind thick windows,
    what are they for?
Monoliths, made up of immortal lines and
    portable ore
can, though unmoved, undergo journeys to a
    different shore.

Here I interject a barrage of wants in
    a devout hush,
stammer in the trickle of one who lacks the
    courage to gush
lest the deluge send to her lips an igno-
    minious blush:
let there be, between the events and me, a
    consonant crush.

When he sees a starry madonna on a
    museum wall,
whisper to him that he possesses lifelong
    freedom to fall;
but when he encounters the vices at a
    devilish ball,

steady him with superimposed shots of the
    loyal and tall.

When, beset by motiveless maladies and
    sorry he came,
he looks at a landscape forlornly and has
    no one to blame
for his vague, unruly unease, instead of
    weeping in shame,
let him take the mood by its ugly throat and
    give it a name.

Last but hardly least, let me share the saintly
    masthead with you:
if one overseer is good for tourists,
    let there be two.
With a backseat license to guide him, there are
    things I'll see through
for the three of us—a successful trip, a
    cell with a view.

Bottom's Dream

Players, are you assembled? Quince is bound and gagged
    and cannot holler "Cut." Two things
are now imperative: that we use our freedom wisely,
    never allowing an upstart ham
to throw the symmetry of our pack seditiously off,
    and that we take advantage of
our newfound liberty, striking the lines we hated—
    the one about the lover's heartache
cutting like glass, for example—and, most fun for us,
    adlibbing where we please. Only
remember the dignity it is incumbent on
    our noble profession to uphold:
beating our breasts, we must have the good sense to know when to stop;
    giving speeches, we cannot abandon
decorum and say what we please, be it ever so moving.
    Are we ready? Then let us leave off learning
our parts and begin our play. Ladies, gentlemen,
    presenting a story of woe, and—so
you know the end right away, the better to grasp the style
    of the piece—lovers and kingdoms restored.
Act One, Scene One. The place: an ancient wall by moonlight,
    somewhere in . . . but what is that shape
moving in the trees, above your painted heads?
    I never saw such golden ringlets,
thought only a speech could strike so suddenly at the heart!
    For God's sake, duck! It disappears,
and I must see where it goes! The show must go on? What show?
    This is better than all our weddings,
sadder than all our deaths combined! The spectacle
    can wait; there will be time enough
for cheap impersonations when the real thing is gone.
    Fair friend, where are you? See what a flawless
jewel it is! Are you real, or a demon sent to haunt me?

Leave my sight and I'll crawl after you;
stay and I'll promise to slay this company of punks.
   It goes. Oh what a sudden distaste
I feel for you all! Go on, complete your dreary drama;
   it has become impossible
for me to take your hijinks seriously, and
   I never liked your kind anyway.
Oh my receding love, oh patron saint of asses,
   grant me the wit to get out of the woods!

Homecoming

Back to the blackened outlines of midsummer.
The little death delays a mightier one.
In the accustomed ruckus of homecoming
fatted limbs, like mechanized tumbleweeds,
roll by the book; but looks can be deceiving.
Anchorites are beasts at the core, and after,
slighted by sleep, I imitate the standard
iconographic renderings of shame:
wild eyes all but gouged out of vision, one hand
clutching a gash of a mouth, the clawlike other
covering what it can. The returning hero
enters the district like a ton of bricks,
and all the sighs that circled for his favor
surface again as howls, offended spirits
forming a club and damned if they will welcome
him as a member. Out the clouded window
they spot a willing helpmate; from that moment
company is nothing but a skinfest,
proffered arms the kneejerks of a patient
eager to keep a well-intentioned doctor
ignorant of a deeper malady.
Once I set up cranial jousts in honor
of the mute mass whose muteness I prefer now
because it lets me think; I wept and sang him
into a gothic corner with pleas and sermons
to the supreme untouchable, the unmoved
mover of my heart. And he relented.
Now, in the lawless maze of what was once an
orderly sequence of long halls and big doors,
I am at loose ends: does this new light shining
just outside signal a gilded angel's
great arrival, or a prisoner's

sighting of a beam that is not there?
(If I had you, here on the carpet, would you
end up a lesser lure than when we started?)
Gold is gold, and cannot be discounted.
This poor loving chump of a fallen idol
sleeps like a baby while I mold and remold
life away from him. May he go on sleeping,
pillowed by the palpitant shell beside him.
With a lunge as reckless as it is silent
and a cold reception gladly expected,
I will venture, into the night, to find you.

II

The Other Stars

Tripartite schemes were all very well
for the builders who held their blueprints firmly
in hand beforehand. What did it matter
if the two vertical poles didn't touch, seemed so
far apart, in fact, that no one who visited the site
could believe the architect's arrogant babble?
Before they knew it, he'd bridged the two poles with a plank.

I have hidden under these structures of
synthetic comfort when the sky was
overcast. I have even hired a claque of
unemployed actors to stand there with me. But speaking
for myself, I find their tentlike charm diminishing.
Over on the next hill is a line of poker-faced upright slabs,
their bases deep in the dirt, their function something else entirely.

II.

I keep seeking this pleasure-giving eye mote;
you fill your pew and my view with
golden uncontrollable emanation
and the music surges in response,
a coded story of hope and disappointment
decipherable to the few. Is it wrong
to be overheated here, or not to have left my coat at the entrance?

The only crime would be *not* to swoon,
to see and ignore you, or brand you a brother
in spotless devotion. Beneath the bleeding windows
hearts must have heft, masses of skin become

human tremors, to feel the force of the organ.
On its own the rite is a starchy obligation;
add intrigue and the altar ripples and ripples.

III.

Over the hub of the hill, a solid wall of
silver leaves. Underfoot, soil without
burrows. Blanketing soil and leaves, a scrim of
hushed and unpunctured blue. Then all of a sudden,
rumors of something about to happen: the night
restless with its own unkeepable secrets,
the very air strained and achingly electric.

Because you are not here, nighttime behaves
this way, calling for terms I'd long since put away:
susurration, intrigue, reverberant. It is only
in your magnanimous absence that stony surroundings
can sing your praises so; I curse even as I gape
to know that their raving requires your being
anywhere else. The evening hums in compensation.

IV.

His beak is open as if in mid-worm or
mid-sentence, his feet impressively sturdy as they
straddle the street. What gives him away,
though, is the magenta pool spreading rapidly
under his otherwise unruffled stomach.
Something ended this bird so suddenly that
he never had time to strike a normal death pose.

It would be overdone and untrue
to say I am the bird, to paint myself in similar terms
as stunted, irretrievably downed, forever rooted
to unkind ground. It would smack of self-pity.
We are partners instead beneath a general rubric
of doom: an arrow descended and brought
him, startled, to death, me screamingly to life.

    V.

I loved a statue and watered it daily.
Sooner or later it softened and let me
break a vital part of it off;
with my hard-won prize in my pocket
I explored the streets with a secret,
but before long the plundered piece was
dust in my hands, and painful to look at.

Now another effigy makes me
shudder at its criminal threshold.
More than ever I entertain a
shameless urge to steal or caress it,
but the facts of history tell me
otherwise: you get what you pray for
and the statue dwindles to rubble.

    VI.

Although others lack the sharpened knives
to be villains, they do what they can with
blunter instruments. Sparring to kill time,

falling to fisticuffs when eloquence evades them,
they get their day's entertainment from
instruction manuals bought at auctions; when one
utters his bored "Touché," a gaggle of fans surround him.

How much deadlier is your collection of
swords with a history, scimitars that glint
even when strung up and inactive. Although I would gladly
lay a whetstone at your door for one blinding night of
thrust-and-parry, you have no need of
anything resembling aid: one twist of your weapon
outstabs the meanest ranks of dullard soldiers.

VII.

The avuncular figure with grizzled beard,
the bearer of balm for the stricken and
abandoned, the craggy but spirited sickle-carrier
paces the page of a long-forgotten book of days
and never once frowns. There is no need to:
our days may be numbered, but . . . (and here his eyes
mist over with comforting thoughts of gold and rainbows).

His evil twin wants none of this waiting,
this starry-eyed torpor. Hoping to scare eternity
into submission, he too brandishes a sickle, but
everything goes wrong: he pierces his own leg and must go
on crutches. Before long, he falls into childish fits
of self-pity, proffering sickle and leg to hirelings,
saying "Lop it off, boys, and be quick."

VIII.

During the first stages of frenzy, a glut of
meaning descends on nature. As if to spite cynics
who call dirt nothing but dirt, terrific breezes
mere conveyors of pollen, something in the
sufferer's mind seeks out and finds corroboration
in vast planets and puny insects: all are as prone to
nervous tics, all whirring with badly kept secrets.

Time passes, and the system turns on you. When
all is sacred, nothing is safe: silent lampposts suddenly
pipe up in irresistible colloquy a tone too high, the sky
calls you but does not want your replies, and
water-bound birds decline pronouns in Latin. It is a hotbed
that cannot stand the addition of an offending
presence; it whispers until you are well on your way.

IX.

Before you came on the scene and blasted
the image to bits, I thought of love as a
spacious courtroom where evidence was presented
graphically and up front, where deserving plaintiffs
got what they wanted legally, and where
judges beamed beneath picturesque wigs when they saw
happy verdicts amicably arrived at.

These days, law is something to be left at the door
along with galoshes; I spend my nights in sinister
mock-trial, playing all the parts. "Guilty or not?"
booms our pot-bellied, exquisitely bored judge. I answer

for you: "Not, your holiness; this harridan framed me."
And then I object. And then, hunched over in a corner
of the courtroom, a juror suggests we all go out to lunch.

    X.

It was a run of the mill journey until the windows
seemed to have melted; outside the train,
the foliage of early summer received an
instantaneous drenching. Startled, I thought of you
like a lovesick heroine out of an old romance:
"Holding her heart, agawp at nature's rages,
she would watch the storm from inside, and secretly like it."

No longer the dainty hand-to-the-head, the tragic
meaningful stare out the window. No storm buffets
alone; however stunningly leaves may shudder and
press against the pane, it is a wasted downpour if
nobody comes out soggy. Reaching my stop, I
left my cap and trenchcoat inside a locker
and headed for the wet jungle, hot on your heels.

    XI.

Our meeting is as stiff as a long-dead thoroughbred.
Like its former coat, we too are glossy and brief;
no frizzy wire springs up that is not
dutifully cropped; our every neigh is strictly
by the book; place us in a lineup of
similarly frozen stallions, and you will not know
one rigor mortis from another and another.

I could endure a salvo of kicking, a brutish uprearing
nag, or a vicious race to the finish, over this
wingless duo of moribund mares. I could even
stand it if you leapt up and started poking holes
in my horse metaphor. Anything other than the way
our speech resembles the two extremes of stunted growth:
gorgeous stillborns, cynical has-beens. This is no time for pleasantry!

XII.

I have been dreaming you into the picture
when you bound, unseeing, past me. I tingle
onward with knees of jelly, glad
to be confirmed in my scheming: this walk
is no hopeless ramble, but a perfect way
of seeing and being seen. Fate, sensing
my hopes, obligingly guides you outdoors.

What rankles is the time it takes me
to realize that you are truly, tangibly here.
I have been holding so many secret meetings with you
that this brief encounter, this perfect opportunity
passes, doesn't register. I see you in retrospect:
you were here, jacket flapping in the noon breeze,
and gone by the time I had presence of mind to grasp it.

XIII.

Explaining camouflage: a useful way
of suiting yourself to your habitat so that
you steal its features more than it steals yours; in war,

a surefire method of avoiding skirmishes;
in love, a vanishing act that lets you watch the object
of your affection, in whose vagrant eyes
you might as well be a pebble, a flaw on the leaf.

Or, a ruinous self-effacement, brainchild
of the timid, deserving to be trounced
by the rustle in the trees which announces
a vital presence, the force which, storming a fortress,
subjects its tenant to a scrutiny of his most
cherished beliefs, the stunning hybrid
you look at once and cannot get out of your mind.

    XIV.

Hearing you praised is enough to make my
overbaked brain a warpath for feuding
goddesses. Only instead of swords,
their messages clash, each one a model of
what I might do. On one side, Silence,
stately in black, shows no sign of unrest;
her only response to the beaming crowd is to nod.

On the other side in see-through red, a goddess
named Outrage deafens her rival with laudatory
overdrive; next to her encomia both clean
and unclean, the excesses of the laurel-throwers
positively begin to pale. It is her manner that
somehow filters out; the walls start to rumble, the floorboards,
feeble at keeping secrets, murmur "Swear it."

XV.

In the handed-down inventory of love's habits
we find images of lowering: down at the mouth,
down on the knees, prostrate with the shock of the marvelous.
Contact more than shame-faced with the elevated figure
is therefore impossible; hazard more
than a bow, and a trapdoor opens beneath you;
offer a hand, and see love disappear.

There is never a mention of the sudden boost
the run-down ego receives when, flinging a jest
from toad-high levels, it witnesses more than
haughty approval. Nor is it told how the jest
(some minor impromptu line) gets told and retold
in the prolonged wake of the moment; seraphs laugh at it,
trees love it; you see your dullness shine in another's eyes.

XVI.

A dream straight out of a textbook: having been
tied up and pointed at the wall by a swarthy, hairy-
faced thug and her henchmen, I hear the incredible shouts
as an old babysitter is disemboweled.
Severed organs flap to the floor like pancakes,
but I do not think "Me next," fearing instead
that it will fall on me to clean up the horrible mess.

What can I do, on waking, but clench my stomach
in sharp, instinctive need to keep it closed?
In wars between the hirsute and the nurturing, nobody
dares to cheer for the former, though her company, being

moody, is hellishly more alive. Will this day or
the next bring pearly surfaces to the brink of
spilling over? (Somewhere the babysitter screams your name.)

XVII.

Once a day, you report to the resident loony
for clues leading to the whereabouts of
the author of a love letter you have received.
She is mad but useful, delving as she can into
alternate worlds; and as you grill her from the other
side of the bars, a strange bond begins to form
between you. She seems to have felt as you do.

Little do you know that this sibyl is also a relentless
self-promoter. She ladles out counsel ("You can tell
she wants to be tracked down") and misinformation
("I think I know where she lives") like a watery broth
that keeps you coming back for the meaty pay-off
at the bottom. All this you realize and tolerate,
never suspecting that she's the one you want.

XVIII.

When you are within shouting distance it is
no matter, or next to none, what you say or
whether we speak at all. It is enough
to see, and covertly to love, your bright array of
colorful traits. They are no sooner parceled out than
stored up, secret accounts to be gone over until
the whole single-spaced ledger is memorized.

But when you leave, ledgers cannot contain you;
time passes and the beloved blurs, the riotous gestures
fade in substance, though not in force. I cannot hear
your voice if I try; and what do I do when
a free-floating affection outraces its
visible target? From your splendid outpost
that dazzles merely by being yours, send photos.

XIX.

Abroad, you are a mass of extra shadow
falling on all you see. On its own a square
is stiff and formidable; walk in it and
the arches tremble, the smells from the canal
soften and linger. The red of the hills
at evening is fit for a postcard home, until
you step in the picture—and hand it back to the masters.

It is straight out of a shoddy French novel
to squeeze the continents into us/them
categories and chapters—mold here, fruit there,
stubble in places and wheat in others. Think me less
a philistine when I say how little the steps
of the journey frame you. It is you, torchbearer to
shrouded lands, who flood them with living color.

XX.

When I call you to mind, you respond sluggishly
if at all. It is as if, being busy, you send
a very expensive mannequin in your stead,

a robot who dresses and walks like you but
cannot capture your puzzling essence. Memory
loves paradox: the more I require a stand-in,
the looser the seams, the phonier the puppet.

But I do not know this until the unexpected happens.
Sifting my horde of jewels and praising their cut,
I come upon a diamond that puts them to shame;
catching a glimpse of familiar patterns of color
in the street, I realize the cheapness of the household dolls
I have been thinking about, relieved that even now,
surprises like this put you fleetingly back in the picture.

XXI.

It will be objected that in missing you I forfeit
a key to the room reserved for bona fide lovers.
There, an air of resolute calm prevails: it is always
"Our minds are as one, and that is enough,"
or "I saw him last night in the shape of a cloud,"
or, harder still to believe, "Look at the
useful machine I built instead of grieving."

They may brace themselves and speak of the
salubrious sublime; they may grit their teeth and
bear it; their tourniqueted hearts are as
undone as mine. Away, you are no
homing compass or dove, but a roving, ceaselessly
altering scoundrel. To miss you is to miss
the loot you add to your repository of noises.

XXII.

Horses, birds, babysitters and jails,
shadows, churches and trains; one would think
you'd sat up with me all night, filling out forms
on what images you preferred, or at least been
consulted in the matter. Failing that, one might suppose you
to have stood on the sidelines in mounting horror
as, one by one, strange pictures of you took flight.

But you stumbled into this mess of blocks
like the bumbling idiot in a screwball
comedy. Center stage contained cardboard boxes
you tripped over before smiling and
wandering on, in your madcap way, to new scrapes.
Meanwhile, the whirligig thrives in your absence: booted cubes
swoon for their muse, a poltergeist in a bowtie.

XXIII.

A spider loved a bee and, knowing that to trap him
would be to kill him, devised webs just flashy enough
to keep the insect guessing. And soon,
seeing in the spider's handiwork traces
of his own flower-hopping, the bee came
closer. Arachnid vapors wafted over them as
the bee proposed to die in the spider's service.

"No!" screamed the latter, tightening up her floss,
and the spurned bee flew on to more accustomed
turf—roses and lilies next to whom (he saw)
the spider was nothing. But she was not so lucky.

The web she'd spun for him got tangled
in her post mortem antenna-flailing, and finally wound
around her neck and choked her. It was the end of the fable.

XXIV.

The more love grows, the bigger its sealed-off
palace becomes, and the more pinched and dark its
stoical keeper. Inside, sun breeds space: a ray
that snuck past the keeper enters a room and lights it—
only now there is not one room but many.
Beams bright as lasers but gentler give away
the safe behind the painting, the corridor under the rug.

If only the keeper, hardened by circumstance,
could learn from this endless illumination
and turn the room inside out. Light would then
seep through leathery skin, giving its secrets away
in a gradually spreading glow, turning skin the orange
of pure beatitude. But there are only two options for the keeper:
to be charbroiled all at once or eternally silent.

XXV.

Then, any enterprise requiring new clothes
was privately hissed, if openly hailed;
too close to a floral militia thinking as one
were the standard frills, the required rustles,
and thinking myself a beacon among dark ladies,
I called the clothes by their hidden agendas:
ethical corsets, trusses of the spirit.

Now I cry out for the colorful front
of fancy dress, bow down in belated awe
before silk and organza. It is not the delusion
of being at my best, but the promise of further
secrecy that thrills me; these veils only make
unveiling all the stranger and wilder,
and under my gown claw ghosts you'll never see.

XXVI.

This sideshow of outlandish images
is nothing like the main attractions of
another time. Just after one picture clicks on
and the eyes have adjusted, another, altogether
different one takes its place, and another, and another.
What in the world is going on? Did the projector
gather together the uppermost slides on the pile?

Nothing could be falser. It is only that
the replacement of the reel calls for as many
tricks and turns as possible to be an even
passable substitute. Everything is its field;
its lens is a gaping hole with a passion for
things encyclopedic. This is the only way
it can capture your many angles—small comfort, yet comfort still.

XXVII.

The next time our paths cross there will be
none of this shilly-shallying, this bondage,
like it or not, to fickle time, brute locale.

The crossing itself will slow down the march
of the passing moment with its own
unstoppable steam, its tenebrous and sultry
collection of vapors. It will be love in a bottle.

But there is always a screw loose somewhere,
a gap in the glass that lets in a limber
array of interlopers. From the mutual friend
who smells a levity and wants in, to the premature bonging
of the hour, to the false confines of the walls
of our houses, there is always a damnable flaw
in the system . . . and incoming elves who taunt "Excuses, excuses."

XXVIII.

What it is about this flame I label passion
that burns the world and its newspapers to a crisp?
How can I call myself hungry for facts of one kind
but wince at another? The lover's room may be an
all-white, tiny room with a view of woods, but why,
if a well-meaning friend slides a special report
under my door, do I look for tongs and a furnace?

Because the flame is not only self-infatuated,
given to burning documents for the sake
of flaunting its own reds, but also in a state
of permanent warfare; all worldly
flare-ups, all currencies not its own, remind it
that amid the worst incendiary horrors, it goes on
stoking itself for want of a proper spark.

XXIX.

The catechism of the far gone: isn't it too good
to be coincidental that our eyes have looked at that
billboard with the same unqualified disgust?
Can we ignore the fact that you happened
to witness the accident only minutes after I did?
Is there more than just a flimsy link in
a story jointly loved, a pastime avoided?

No, yes, and by no means. These are the very
traits which, observed in an enemy, get
shelved or denied by their once proud possessor.
I could pillage an igloo, travel to the torrid
antipodes and produce thousands like you,
featured like you, like you in raves and complaints.
I was bedazzled by a ray of fool's gold.

XXX.

Go, tyrant. In your heart will nest
no more desperate slaves. Come again, days
of productivity, nights of rest and no nightmares.
I have spent so much time under the shade
of your massive umbrella that I will draw it shut
for a minute to see what I once saw, and what I have
missed since seeing you. Eyes, look unchained around you.

It is a landscape of moldering stones and bones.
When the eyes are free to roam, they are not
so much free as useless—I see a sky of
fledgling clouds and do nothing to help them,

peer into the living record of a severed oak and can
decipher nothing. Return, dark glasses, come again,
morbid parasol; only in shade do mountains have features.

XXXI.

In the final tally of divine overseers
who will be ours? Suppose we claim
the moon, whose bottomless bag of stardust
enchants a forest of two, softens and
shrinks the volume of venomous air
between us, and lovingly coats all former fears
with beams of forgetful, nourishing light?

Our watcher is the moon, but only after a brutal
shake-up is through with her. She has never learned
the knack of lighting two people at once; instead
it is always me illumined, you off in the bushes,
you posed in your halo, me waist-deep in darkness.
And she is a clumsy goddess for the reason
that she borrows (poor moon) what light she has from me.

XXXII.

Though you are by definition a slippery freedom,
if forced to freeze you in a single image
I would call you a beam of light with hidden powers
to strike and alter forever. Here is a room:
regard its monotone grimness. Enter your
incandescent highness: gladly around you
objects sparkle, knowing a beam when they see it.

Next to your flawless arc I am a damaged
bulb in a fleabag hotel, clattering on to reveal
paintings on velvet and *objets trouvés* (but where?),
rattling off to plunge the run-down room into
dark desuetude. What if we pooled our forces?
Would we stand together like heartless neon sculpture
or deck ourselves in loving chiaroscuro?

XXXIII.

Perfect, you say? It is enough to make me perform
operations on myself in order to test your love:
taking in the wreckage, you would be forced to say
"Yes, gouging out one eye makes the other shine
all the brighter; the smell of your fungus reminds me of summer;
your leprous stump is a modish charmer
since, after all, green is my favorite color."

And yet, for all our tirades against deception,
how easily do we succumb to the lover's flattery,
and with what treachery. If I am perfect, it is only
by being perfect that you, myopic, dependable you
can keep me; so go on, keep on calling me faultless, come on,
hurry up with my supper, leave me, and come back at midnight,
but don't come back if you hear a noise in the room.

XXXIV.

Still the inveterate skulker, the ghost
of chaos past, I have come back to the place
where it all began, where leaving, you gave me

leave to see you wherever I went—
in the home, in the wild, in the sky, in the gutter—
and where columns, scribbled on and abandoned,
took one look at my raving, and rose again.

Strangest of all is that, given the chance
to see my subject in the fabulous flesh at last,
I would flatly refuse. These barren days
when I heat my room by the fading coals of my goals,
this ache for an ache is as good as it gets,
so go on running; I will go on looking for you
as the willow bends, as the stomach hunts for the ulcer.

III

Question and Answer

I.

Why walk in the eye of a private tornado,
looking as if your life depended on taking cover
sooner rather than later? Why stare at the sky
as though a high-flying dirigible with your name on it

were getting closer? Not to pound your spirit
into bloated pulp, not to reach an abyss and stay there,
certainly not to shoot your head off, but rather
to screw it on tighter, to be able to say

that your stint as victim of molten pavements
is an exercise in pushing vision to the limit
and pulling it back again, a way of proving
that the swiftly approaching dirigible is not there

and has no name on it, and that you are braving
a lesser Avernus, harrowing man-made hurdles
at your own smart pace, high and mighty enough
to smuggle the sun, then nudge it back into place.

II.

Why talk about your affliction so little,
when there are so many stricken faces
waiting to quiz you, so many sympathetic places
where you can lay your cards on the table?

Over by the stream, a scar festival is in progress.
One girl circles her wound with a blood-red marker;
another, ambitious, has chosen her outfit
to show her gash in all its festering greatness.

One man even opens his stitches with a jackknife
to the cries—"Stunning!" "Cheating!"—of the other contestants.
Then a judge hands out prizes. How much better
to be over in the workaday bleachers

shyly subscribing to the doctrine of publish
and perish, happily letting your wild eyes
and barely discernible limp elude the judges
while you waste away in the arms of a purer terror.

   III.

Why work so hard at putting your throes down,
when walking so much and talking so little
get you far enough? Why build meddlesome shackles
for the spirit that, phoenixlike, always rises

out of rude, embarrassing ash? Because more often
than not, the world's most confident fliers are compulsive
liars—the bracing walk was a cripple's invention,
the oath of silence only meant the beak's owner

suffered from lockjaw, and the wings you relied on
were taped on and getting set to fall off,
at which point, in came voices from the sidelines
who treated you to a flurry of reportage

until, sturdier than it ever had been,
prettier than it could ever truly be, the new-made bird,
hard as a rock and encrusted with diamonds,
flew off to its enduring, winged victory.

Three Songs

I.

I was in the bookstore, reading the ends of mysteries,
when the gunshots went off just outside.
I was in the drugstore, seeking delicious remedies,
when the leper shuddered at my side.

In a world where love is innocent and upstanding,
sicknesses and riddles are over soon,
but when love is real, the universe starts expanding
like a crazy, out-of-control balloon.

How to know the brave new moves from the same old motions?
How to tell the first from the thirteenth prize?
By the stricken heart's obliviousness to potions,
by the awful magnitude of surprise.

II.

The threnodist stopped his story in mid-sentence:
why were all the listeners looking down,
each pair of eyes encased in its own sorrow,
each pair of lips contorted in a frown?

The famous beauty entered the room expecting
a loud response, an episode of violence,
but to her great annoyance, all her suitors
stared at the walls in unprotesting silence.

Bearers of bad news would like nothing better
than to raise a purgative, public moan,

but a communal feeling is a false one:
genuine grief must run its course alone.

III.

The eyes that start a fire in his head,
the heart that skips a beat for him alone,
the smiles that tingle up and down his spine
would get you somewhere if they were your own.

But someone always hovers in the room
where you and your enchanted one embrace;
look up from hot and bothered limbs to see
a jealous warden with an angel's face.

He gives you all the gorgeous words of praise
that he will give another and another,
but when he finds a phrase he really likes
he holds his tongue and saves it for his mother.

Parables of Flight

I. Out of the dovecote they come—the confident flappers, the cliques who must travel in v's, the ones who initially wheeze but sooner or later outsoar their brashest colleagues. As they fly, an underground spy sees them, wriggles out of his hole and into his bush disguise, and heads for the forest. He waits. When they pass over, he shoots. Some, struck in the heart, fall at once and are placed in his bloody sack. Others are wounded in less delicate places—a wing, a leg—and take shelter in the nearest treetop, where they nurse themselves, a few with success. But there is always one bird who hears the blast and, far enough behind to see his friends falling, hides until the shoot-out is over. Then he staggers back to the dovecote, where the ghosts of his dead and dying friends hover around him like nagging schoolboys, saying do it right this time, fool the assassin with your suavity and know-how. And the memory of their bodies flying—beaks held arrogantly high, stomachs taut and ready for anything—makes him hobble to the window and look out longingly.

II. What is the rule that says pain has a correlation? What is this flutter of images running together—blood to the head, birds to the sky; red in the cheeks, flocks up from trees, out of hiding? I do not know why they fly as they do, only that it is high time I was one of their party again.

III. The sea slug had grown so used to her daily ooze down the shoreline that she did not twitch a muscle when she saw the fantastic seabird wading in the water. Coolly she met his avid gaze; his plumage was not for her. But the seabird mowed her down; they tussled; she screamed; he vanished. The sea slug grew fatter and fatter until one day, quite unnoticed among the jellyfish and the sea anemones, there came into the world a memory of the scuffle, a winged worm.

IV. It is as much for treading firmly on the ground as it is for taking leave of my senses. Only with this condition: as I walk, I must have an overhead lens cap aimed at me. Eagle, madman or missile, it does not matter. So long as someone is watching.

V. A nightmare transcribed: downed by a sudden cramp or stealthy torpedo, I lie bleeding on the grass. Two vultures come out from behind a tree with a stretcher and make their way toward me. I do not protest, but tumble into the cool white fabric. The vultures then cart me offstage to a distant infirmary, where nurses monitor my every whimper, and tales of exultant whippoorwills speed my downfall. The grass looks better without me.

VI. Cloud, be my messenger. Soak up the pool outside my window and carry it over fences and forests to the sorrowful house where my loved one waits. You will recognize it by the candle burning in the window. Do not delay! Those other puddles will muddy the message, keep you from getting there fast. Carry, cloud, my love exclusively, over the millions of lifeless clouds, under a guiding invisible hand. Why do you stop? Is it need for fuel that makes you drink the dregs from beer mugs, absorb those waters better left alone? Oh greedy cloud, how much more can you hold? How much longer can the candle burn? Now you have done it. I do not know whether your belly put out the candle, or whether sudden darkness made you lose your way and panic, but either way, cloud, we're doomed.

VII. A nod; she's smiling. A smile; she's soaring. There is no better way of causing hope to plummet than seeing another poor gull fly the same way, watching a swallow alight in another's eyes.

VIII. "Would you mind looking these over?" "Not at all." "This is the wingspread, these are the colors I like, and this is how we start it." "Ingenious. Would you like some water?" "No, thank you, I'm fine. What problems, if any, do you foresee with the plans?" "None. You've worked it all out admirably. Go ahead and build it." "Don't you think it will be hard to get the materials?" "Improvise!" "Have you ever flown, I mean really flown?" "I traveled to India last year, and next week I go to Rome." "But is it enough?" "What do you mean?" "Is it hot in here?" "No."

Mirror Effects

I. The Philosopher's Lamp
(after Magritte)

The man is smoking his own nose! Into the pipe
it goes, a mighty snout if there ever was one,
and all appears fixed and finished until,
entering the frame again,
the nose creeps up a table
where it serves as a candle which lights
the room, making possible our knowledge
that the man is smoking. . . .

                 What if my leavings
are like his poor misguided ravings, fuel for my own
pleasure, illumination, but nonetheless
based on my circulation, and therefore
getting me nowhere fast? Pressing questions, but
smoking is never really the same as stroking—
the nose, the passion puts us to work,
the flame collides with air before we inhale.

II. The Binge

After a big meal, the gourmand retires
and feels her body gloat: from the first dainty sip
to the final, ravenous bite of the eclair,
course after course was nearly perfect
and now they course through her stomach, turning
that staid cavity into a churning
carousel of pleasure; but when the body revolts,
the gourmand feels the food take its toll
and cannot get up!

Just as, slinking to her room
in woozy contentment, sinking into a chair
whose lushness is nothing next to her visions,
smirking her way through loaded questions
(what is action? the work of the lonely;
what are friends for? making the day pass)
and counting the boundless ways of the heart—
full, like a fat girl's plate, to bursting—
the satisfied lover cannot budge an inch.

III. Correspondences

A message is delivered across town:
before a blue box swallows it up, it is pelted
by sodden leaves; taken and placed in an
outdoor bin, it blows into an alley, where it is mistaken
by cats, for a white rat, by dogs, for a hydrant;
it skitters back, but the clerks in the office are eating
chocolate; the postman is mauled by a rabid
housewife; and so it arrives, the original tear-stains
the least of its problems. . . .

The journey from mind
to mouth is no less tortuous, making a heartfelt
passionate speech the target for sins of commission
(a bold idea tamed and disfigured)
and omission (the dwarf who normally mans
the motors is fast asleep and cannot be woken).
As with that cryptic letter you recently received
you must learn to shun the surface,
to draw conclusions when I open my mouth and choke.

Looking at Clouds

In my mad haste to get where I was going
I had almost forgotten the dazzle of clouds
at early evening. Look at that plump one there
pursuing that lonely sliver of a thing—
he lunges, she drifts, she drifts, he follows. But
gruff though he seems, he is gentle to the core
and cannot be called a normal cloud; not for him
the weekly broods over picnics, the spiteful visits
to sun-worshipping cities, the stubborn refusal
to rain on scorched earth and empty reservoirs.
Not for him the brutal need to accost
the sliver and make her part of his own tufty,
overfed self. It is only that, having seen
the partner he wants, he hurries to her side
and will not take no for an answer. Think, he tells her,
of the stir we will make by careening together—
the novel shapes, the heart-stopping sunsets. Consider
the earth's rare blend of envy and awe when it sees us
billowing past. Know that beneath my burly
facade, a birdlike heart is breaking. And look!
She has accepted, and lets him coast beside her!
They cover the sun so that they can be alone,
and their love creates an explosion: giant banners
of red flapping above them, fangs of orange
below them, golden daggers heading east,
mysterious purple blots in the west. Now darkness
permits a bolder embrace, and sudden rainfall
tells us they are flourishing, married by moonlight.
We would do well . . . my darling, where have you gone?

To a Passerby

(after Baudelaire)

Evening spread its shadow on the rooftops;
couples, all smiles, stood smitten on each corner,
feasting on their own eyes. And then it happened:
out of the teeming night there came a mourner—
for a dead friend or his own life, I dared not
guess, but he looked so stricken that I turned
from my own friend's vise-like embrace and stared, not
out of abhorrence, but in fascination,
and then he met my gaze, serenely, proudly!
We should have fled at once, and we both knew it,
but we both lacked the stamina to do it;
tugged by two loves, society and sorrow,
we drifted off to different romances,
leaving behind a monument of glances.

Monologue for a Matron

First one damnable white curtain, then the other
lifts. My vigil was not in vain. His right eye, right hand
the moon lights; the rest she leaves for me to fill in. His very breathing
doubles my heartbeat—not bad for an old taboo,
though the sound may be only the willows swaying. All wrinkles
    and scales,
I have hidden behind a bush. Shall I surprise him on the parapet?

It would go something like this: alighting on the parapet
I find fireworks in the arms of a youthful other.
Caution takes flight, fates frown, and somewhere the scales
of propriety teeter and readjust, but there is no one on hand
to cluck a tongue, wag a finger, or shout "Taboo!"
nor are the willows audible over our breathing.

But if willows can weep, think of the cries of men. Try breathing
in, out, old girl. Would that the rest of me . . . but see him leaning
    over the parapet,
perfect and pure as milk. In, out would mean his downfall, my
    certain lockup. A taboo
holds for a reason. Leave him to pierce another,
nearer bush with his igneous eyes and arrows, and let them go hand
    in hand
past the curtains and pull them shut again. A criminal who scales

a strictly forbidden ladder dandles the scales
of reality until they break; credible shapes begin breathing
that cannot possibly live. But on the other hand
(I have three, each with agile fingers, and am valued at parties),
    a parapet-
snubbing, do-gooding hider in bushes, though loved in high places,
    commits another
crime: the shame of routing out temptation, bowing before taboo.

This is the only villainy worthy of handcuffs. Taboo
or no, a hag in the making sloughs off her scales
when she mounts a challenge and steers it to the other
side of the great gulf, past signs marked "Stay out," or "Keep your
    breathing
normal, your lust spectral and below-board." Still on the parapet,
immaculate tyrant? Looking for something? I could hand

you letters written in a crabbed and passionate hand.
I could wait until, taking it into your own head to turn taboo
to the winds, you descended from the parapet.
I could do many things. But when my hardened scales
quicken and itch to be touched by more than your breathing,
my feet get ready to climb. I can do no other.

First one tentative groping hand, then the other
starts to scale the wall. Taboos were made to be broken.
You hear me breathing on the parapet, and come closer.

Stage Directions for a Short Play

In sweet-smelling room of expensive clutter
roué sits in oversized armchair, thinking.
Languorously sighs, languorously rises,
opens the window,

shuffles back to seat. Sudden clap of thunder
jolts him; instantaneous rush of rainfall
turns his sturdy chair to a shipwrecked boat, his
reverie somber.

Widens eyes as water and still more water
charges in; regarding a bare wall downstage,
notices a larger than life-sized shadow
made by her passing.

Water, wind and dust become fighting fragments
of a spinning, vertical tunnel; all the
nooks in the interior are now damaged
past recognition;

vases fly; silk garments begin to flutter,
then are blown, in sopping-wet scraps, around him.
Roué clutches armrests and shivers in his
nakedness; curtain.

Venus Observed

When she came to shore, it was not the perfect occasion
it came to be labeled. Some said her starry expression
sprang not from dumbstruck wonder over being born
but from total confusion; poised as she was
between one bad place (couples insanely grabbing
each other, pink flowers flying any which way)
and another (a shore whose appointed handmaiden
and lines of upright trees promised balmy days
of doing things by the book), what could she do
but keep her glassy eyes forward, stalling
by seeming dazed? Others noted
that the V-like perturbations in the water
could be understood as the sea's way
of taking her stillness to task: "Venus, Venus,"
the ripples seemed to say, as if the burden
of choosing weren't heavy enough already.
But whoever was right, and her nearness to shore
notwithstanding, there was no next frame and
she stands there still, considering all her options—the winds
serenade her, the priggish handmaiden foists clothing
upon her, and all she can do is turn
to her audience asking for pity, for someone's help
in deciding: brute elements or bland shore?
Perhaps her wisest option is to stand there forever,
smiling her vacant smile; having neither side
has kept her dreaming of both, and by now she is far,
far gone, happy in a world with ample room
for storms and schedules, and not this seascape
of necessary evils, love on the half shell.

Young Love

After their first electric conversation
she bolted to her room, and he to his;
colorful sparks and shapely images
brightened their thoughts with new illumination—

cursing her appetite, whose lustful motive
gobbled up all her efforts to be proper,
blessing her stubborn tendency to stopper
sentiment with dry wit, she set up votive

candles in her own honor. He in his turn
blazed with the brilliant role he had created;
scholarly, stern, but dying to be dated
when the right moment came, he let a flame burn

until it looked like ardor. Both had groundless
reasons for love, although they called it boundless.

Night hurried off with what the day had woven,
dreams showed the happy pair where they were heading.
In a deserted valley he lay bleeding
while a repulsive animal with cloven

hooves and familiar features leapt around
in a balletic swoon, then fired an arrow
(which had been dipped in sugar) at a sparrow
who faltered, then fell, lifeless, to the ground.

That this was heaven there was no mistaking,
but a long wait revealed her residence
as a cloud to whose lofty eminence
nobody traveled. Both awoke and, shaking,

pondered a painful quandary: should love
settle for hell below, or hell above?

Menacing shadows colored their next meeting,
although the scene was passionate enough,
made up primarily of harmless fluff:
she called him "heaven sent," he called her "sweeting."

But before long, she dropped the fatal bombshell:
wouldn't a loving merger cost too much?
Two lines so similar could never touch,
two restless yolks would squirm inside one eggshell.

Moved, he agreed: why meddle with perfection?
She was his angel and he was her savior.
Sully their love with bestial behavior
and the spoiled egg would barely pass inspection.

He was in tears, and she was broken-hearted.
Hastily, and with relief, they parted.

Drinks in the Town Square

No sooner had they carried their martinis
over to the café's remotest table
and huddled close to praise the coming sunset,
red as a famous letter, than it happened:
empty when they had entered it, the square now
quivered with life. What she saw: burly spinsters,
big books in hand, refusing to be selfless,
women in white and, lurking in the shadows,
elegant lady spies. What he saw: strutting
romeos, hearts for rent, devoted scholars
for whom high windows could outshine rich widows,
cynics for whom all cities were the same.
They had come all this way, by plane, by marriage,
hoping to pit their love—with all its thriving,
colorful avenues, unending crops—to
everything else, but now the square was teeming
with all the faces they had left behind!
Visitors from their own obstructed futures
dazzled their eyes and scarred their hearts much more than
glamorous strangers they could never have,
and when the square began to reassemble
they butted heads and called each other darling,
as if to cover private crimes with public
blandishments. But there was no denying
that each grinning face was a murderer.
When all the ghosts got up and walked out, they were
left with a vivid sense of screen doors closing,
and when they staggered homeward, there were trembling
fists in their pockets, daggers in their eyes.

Dinner at Le Caprice

How good it would be if our surroundings always
mirrored the kindest contours of our hearts,
if the unimpressive restaurant at whose table
the couple sit and stammer were named Le Caprice
and if, made braver by each successive glass
of golden potions, abetted by the kind of waiter

who looked as if he were born to be a waiter—
tall and perfectly two-toned—they promised always
to dine together; shattering all the glass
in the place with the high-pitched singing of their hearts,
pitching their flag between the camps of caprice
and earnestness, they would join hands across the table

as their feet careened and twisted under the table
to the visible astonishment of the waiter,
in whose cynical opinion what starts as caprice
ends in disaster, but who revises what he always
says when, noting their keen eyes and steadfast hearts,
he takes a photo and puts it behind glass

so that tomorrow's patrons, flicking shards of glass
at each other's throats, will look up from their table
and feel the envy blossoming in their hearts
while in the background the melancholy waiter
thinks aloud, "Love may die, but there is always
one picture-perfect couple at Le Caprice."

But pictures lie, and love is a mad caprice
doomed as fat farm animals, fragile as glass.
The worst imaginary restaurant is always
better than the suggestive carcass, the table

across whose sahara of distance we stare, and the waiter
who shakes his head at the spectacle of two hearts

as tepid and terribly ill-matched as two hearts
can be—one entertaining a bold caprice
to rush out, screaming "Fire!", the other begging the waiter
for tips on conversation and glass after glass
of garnet poisons, and who will be at another table
the next day with the next victim, hoping as always

to do better than the glassy-eyed couple who always
come in, hearts racing, on either side of the waiter
who shows them to their table at Le Caprice.

Worms and Us

I.

Maggots in the food, maggots in the floorboards,
maggots in the recurring nightmare in which,
lying down with a rugged adonis,
I wake to find him almost nibbled away.
Certainly signs of death are everywhere,
but love is more than combat with worms
and cannot be so glibly explained away;
I do not tremble or knock my knees
to keep the maggots slumbering below ground,
or crush them underfoot by flocking to
everything they are not: raucous gatherings,
stolen kisses. On the contrary,
I come away from parties adoring
what is wormlike in them: the unrisen soufflé,
the precocious boy's octogenarian sayings,
the drooping lids of the hostess, someone's
death rattle of a laugh. Certainly love has
commerce with vermin, but it is a friendly
partnership, not a league of discord;
a hacking cough gives proof of a full life,
a passing stranger seems all the stronger
when one foot is sinking quietly into the grave.

II.

But it is this lingering horror of dust
that makes me pull us out of the cold earth
any way I know how: because I strive
for heaven in little rooms, visit you

in order to suck your blood, then spread it
over pipes and daffodils, and shove you
up to the vacant sky, where you hover
like a stone-cold, tedious statue who never dies,
you, poor pawn, are a jack-in-the-box gone haywire,
and I am a grinning humanist with bad dreams.

Dissolving Views

High noon in the park, as the year begins its
onward march to truly infernal weather.
"Is it hot enough for you?" yell the normal,
but on the sidelines

all the lonely hopefuls whose blood is warmer
than their beds have gritted their teeth and gathered
in their finery for another round of
amateur sleuthing.

Wearing a big black hat, which she believes will
add to her mysteriousness, a woman
sizes up her prey, but he's far away; she
looks at him looking

at another, dimly exotic beauty
who—of all the maddening things—is stalking
a resplendent young man whose line of sight she
furtively follows,

hoping to attract his attention. But he
will not be distracted from his own goal and,
riveting his eyes, ogles up another—
wonder of wonders—

man! But still the travesty is not over:
he is looking longingly at the woman
in the hat, attempting to steer her heartache
in his direction,

but in vain. She gives the whole chain a last look
and sits down, fatigued and disgusted, on a

nearby bench; this craven, pathetic horde of
frustrated lovers

is a shame, a waste! Only fools and martyrs
can endure unbearable oaths of silence
at the same time that they are seeing red and
screaming their hearts out.

Why not change her policy and *do* something?
Track her young man down and seduce him silly?
And then she reflects: it is not the way of
spies and romantics.

An Ode to Freedom

While I was sleeping, an invisible gendarme must have tiptoed in and stationed himself beside me. Because now, woken from dreams of liberty into harsh, unwavering daylight, this hulking presence watching my every blink, I am frozen to the spot. I cannot go out and do what I want. And the manic patterns that the maples make on the walls only serve as mocking reminders of the joys of unchecked motion. Was this what Florestan felt when, locked up for treason, he looked up and saw, not a wife, but total darkness rushing toward him? Was Galileo's dungeon peopled with the same cruel shadows and beefy chancellors; was it any comfort to know that he had added to the sum total of available wisdom? Did satirists jailed for adding a moustache to a political poster react this way when their underground caves led nowhere or caved in? Squirmers on the eternal rack, fighters for freedom, sad consequences of brute historical truths, I see now what you have suffered. Denied the right to exit and pursue, I will sit and listen for footsteps I cannot follow. But on catching sight of myself in a mirror—head cocked like a lovesick spaniel, eyes dewy for lack of my master's voice—I am bound to confess an arrogance almost worthy of punishment. There was a certain thrill in finding giant replicas of my minor passion, but I had nothing at stake but a fragile ego, while others were burned at a stake that was all too real. And now that I see the difference, all these satyr-and-nymph obsessions seem like luxuries paid for by blood. Chastened, extremely lucky, I pause in my raving to honor the dead who got me here, not by their fatal examples but by what they left behind: a window whose bars protect me, a door I keep the key to, and a world, all in all, amenable to my progress. Slaves have been chained to rocks from time to time, and tyrants have carved their hearts out, so I may love.

Speech After a Spectacle

The balconies and the ballrooms may have
vanished, but I'm still here, sporting the same
drop-dead outfit, the same pair of eyes that
shut forever just minutes ago. You also,
I notice, remain; while your yawning colleagues
file up the aisles, headed for bed or feasting,
you sit gripping your armrests testily, sweetly
refusing to rise. And you have been so patient tonight
that, frankly, it would be a shame
to disappoint you; so watch me step down
from the heights and make my way toward you.
Now you will finally know I wasn't joking—
these cheeks were reddened by natural methods
and even a genius cannot fake a heartbeat
or summon a tear unmoved. It was you, it was you
who prodded me all along, and for that reason
I offer you no wings past the wings
but an arrow straight to the heart. Do you
start? Do you think that mortals aren't worthy,
that spirals or crashing chords should keep
the barriers mile-high? Like it or not, I'm here now,
live now, and you must make good on
your threats when the villains plotted against me,
your frowns when the slick seducers won me,
your sidelong grins when they went and left me.
You made the moves; it is my turn to haunt you now,
so flee if you will—I will follow. When you wake
at freakish hours, chilled by an open window,
when the barstool next to you seems to be dented,
when your hair is raked by invisible fingers,
take note, unbeliever: I am only seconds away.

Sea Change

Only by the sea are the world's potential maniacs
made to reconsider; an ass looking out
cannot expect a miracle to stare back, but if a lover
languishes in the sea's direction, he'll find himself
mercifully dwarfed; if a madwoman compares her tortuous ebbs
    and flows
to the ancient lapping of waves, she'll know how little
her posturing adds up to; if a school of aspiring painters
crack up and throw their brushes in the air,
a glance at the ocean will reassure them that the search
for perfection is a go-nowhere business, since even their finest hour
cannot equal the sternness of water—however good they may be
at yearning, raving, striving, the sea does it better.

Only yesterday, when blue eyes faced a blue ocean,
there was a sound to rival the roar of the ocean;
its guttural pleas and poignant cheering rose
higher than waves, and when a fringe of seaweed
washed ashore, its tendrils were fingers, its shape
recalled the mind's capacious inside, the way it holds
an electric forest, each little branch a stroke of lightning;
so that this cry of the stomach, this circuit of nerves
came to be louder and much more absorbing
than the storied ins and outs of the tide, or the sand's
pivotal role in making the beach a bigger beach.

Today is as far from overcast as Canada from China,
but only a whole new species of fog could make me
see what I see: while a band of moustached marauders
cut a beach umbrella into bright confetti,
over on the rocks the barnacles rearrange themselves
into sinister shapes, at which point the seascape
becomes a free-for-all; a bottle brings me

messages so unwelcome that I throw it back again,
off in the dunes, nuns and maenads are wrestling,
and down by the shore are two people running,
fooling the eye so well—gay chase or frantic capture?
sea's foam or his shirt's polka dots? her veil or night mist,
rolling in?—that however often I come to the beach
hoping to stare my cares away, there is always
this fabulous couple playing in the surf.

Autumn Polemic

To the saw that says the countryside is a constant
through which intruders drag their inconstant flesh,
I would take a saw of my own; to the great
sage who claims a city's radiant sameness
outlasts the human chronicle of fatigue,
I would present a bottled heart and a road map
asking which woodman is the bigger liar:
the hearty sprinter, knocking the leaves off elders,
or the gray shade who decks the truant seasons
with fake smoke and massive mirrors? Even autumn,
the only season that sets a person thinking
of reddened faces, giddy enslavement to wind,
is threatened on either side by burgeoning spruces,
skimpy poplars; however slow and steady
the cycles of a many-ringed tree appear,
however safe from disaster, there will still be
the leap, the plunge, when forests lie cut and bundled,
there will be fires burning all year long.

Taking to the Hills

If walking, like wine, only abets a sad mood
let's try it, I said, and I did:
over these hills that have never known sorrow
no thoughtful moon passes. Dig until a hill is level, and unearth
only earth. Take pride in knowing the chemical makeup
of rain, the sum total of harmful vapors in any sunset.
For if you must drag in the old lines
about suicidal willows, star's stacked for or against you,
you clutter a limitless, soaring landscape
with your own baggage. Night of love,
day of omens of night, great mountain
of realized hopes, valley where bitter winds
blow the dispossessed into raving lunatics—
what are they but shady projections
of passing whims, vastly oversimplified versions
of something infinitely greater? This vision before you
is nothing but a triad of trees, hills, river,
steadfast and eternal. But soon you start to feel restless
and when, setting out to take a roll of photos,
you note the disturbing absence of a road,
your suavity crumbles: you deafen the sky
and serenade the moon, fall prostrate before pines
saying oh, come back, spirit of the place which,
lifeless without you, blossoms into something
sumptuously more than mediating madness;
come back, massive oaks that await our coming;
to carve initials is to be truly human;
the days are dappled with our passions,
the mountains rise and fall with our glories and follies.

Love's Passing

Our beds are crowded. I am not a guide
beckoning men to greater things, or a potion-
sipping princess with a death wish, let alone a dyed-
in-the-wool seducer always in motion,
gathering swains like flies. Still less
will I deign to be called a fallen star, sunk too low
for resurrection; I am no more the tragic adulteress
than the ever-patient wife who waits by the window,
thinking a breeze her love. And yet to be none
of these things is somehow to be all—
jabbing a specter wakes it up, pierces the one
last fortress left standing with legions of small,
nagging casements that open onto a formidable array
of upstart possible ghosts. Who shall I be today?

Forward, you spineless creature! What's to be gained
by languishing there without reason, without hope?
Why do it? Not, as you think, to mimic a well-trained
spaniel, playing dead until the go-ahead: I mope
as I do to further my own purposes. What but misery
could follow from your complaining? A world aflame;
houses that light up as I pass them; sparkling company
in the darkest of rooms. Then call it some other name!
For love, read "usefulness"; for desperate hope of mating,
read "admittedly minor passion." Supine I may be, stone-cold
I am not, and cannot be so calculating;
this has a will of its own. But yours is gathering mold
by the minute! So, half awake, I eavesdrop on the trouble
already afoot: four-eyes versus lovelorn double.

Outside, the day takes shape: cars honk and hum
in stalled communal anger, children cross the street as they
    have been taught—

holding hands and in rows—and the grubbiest animals come
out of hiding dressed to the nines. It might be thought
that the sounds of things working, the early whirr
of clocks commanding, does terrible things to those who
     think themselves
bravely above such subjects; that love's executioner
is a slate-gray, city-wide office peopled by elves
giving such sentences as "sign on the dotted line,"
"straighten your tie," or "wake up; your fun is over."
But morning is not a killer so much as a dormant mine
awakening, a slap in the face telling any languid lover
the simple facts: while you lie, dreaming up dangers,
your life is kept in order by millions of strangers.

Oh, my latest weakness, meeting your last one made me
cradle my head and do some serious thinking.
I will assert—though liars will upbraid me—
that it is our lot to be forever sinking.
But sinking at random, punctured by the sorriest group
of paltry aquatic rejects a hand could gather? (Your treason
puts me in mind of lapses of my own: the shifty starfish, the troupe
of tough-guy piranhas, the shark who, already out of season,
stabbed with the best of them.) Perhaps we have all drowned
and now take part in an underwater carnival,
falling in love for all the wrong reasons: the liquor we have downed,
the masks chosen to hide our gaping wounds, the jolly animal
suits that cover our weathered bodies, the grinning cave
not to be filled by wassail, weapon or wave.

Voices from the heart of the heartbreak—dear friend:
it's been a pleasure to serve you, but I find
myself growing restless; kindly to mend
is more my style than rudely to rip. Silly blind

one, like it or not, your sight is returning,
your hard-won wisdom a trophy not to be taken
away so easily. Sufferer, your endlessly burning,
tragically frozen insides may have shaken
you badly, but by now aren't your maladies poses,
your throes a little tired? Fellow traveler, my rack
is not as strong as your aching frame supposes;
such is the strength of your spirit that a crack
can sew itself up, and blistering sores get better
before you even know it. Burn this letter.

But if—if, I say—I give in and drop
this role for another, healthier one, where
will all the headaches and outtakes go? If I mop
my forehead and move on, locate the tumor and tear
it out like an unflattering photograph from its surrounding,
prettier pictures, is there no way to keep
the image alive somewhere, the still-pounding,
scarlet heart in a jar to which I can creep
back and wonder over? (This fear is just as keen
as the former suspicion that, because the object of my madness
had no memory of a scene I treasured, the scene
might just as well not have happened, with the result that my
    depths of sadness,
my blissful heights, got lost in the shuffle.) Oh you who know,
when hearts get better, where does the heartache go?

At least I have known the perils of conversion.
I did not see a horse's mouth, or even
its belly, but everywhere I looked, a mighty version
of weaknesses best kept secret, graven
images when what I wanted was rest, relief.
A smile, a glimpse of asymmetrical features;

the world was cock-eyed and good. But then the grief
when shapers of vision turned out to be teachers
of doom, the awful, sinking surprise
when some chance circumstance—footsteps not
where they should be, eyes that wandered also—would prize
the sweetness from the city, revealing it as the hot
and hellish abyss it was. If I am less interesting to meet
at least I can tell my sickness from your street.

If we could only imitate our heroes
I would like to be Daphne in reverse.
Like my accursed original, my face grows
smaller and smaller as my fate gets worse,
and, to prevent events from turning gory,
I become one gigantic living leaf.
But this is where I modify the story:
after the transformation comes relief.
Walking away from forced conversions, brutes know
that recusants are frozen to the spot.
What they have yet to realize is that roots grow
after the worst disaster. On a hot
day or a windy night, I can be seen
earning my laurels, happy to be green.

Finally another day of normal vision:
signs are signs and people wear their own faces.
What were you thinking? It was your ambition
to turn the busiest public places
into one-note, personal temples, but what a relief
to look out the window and see hard hats, stubborn lands
that strenuously resist being twisted by you! Grief
misshapes whatever it gets its paws on; beggars, their hands
outstretched, seem to be saying, "Leave your heartstrings

with me"; trips to the corner newsstand
are forays into a wild world in which you are queen; art brings
your torments speedily home. But finally now you stand
seeing your city as if for the first time, ready to come back
to the world a new person, until your next attack.

Coming Back to the Cave

Coming back to the cave is when the hard part
begins. What can be said to your bosom companions
the howling mouth, the thumb-twiddler and the dim-witted
    rhapsode
that cannot be translated into one cruel sentence:
I have been there, envy me? In the thick of the
ignorant night, icicles clinging ever more
stubbornly to the walls, what can be done
to bring the sunlight in? It would be easy
to fashion earplugs out of worn-out clothing,
to striate the walls with a record of hated days,
to pare down one's speech to a one-note lament
of long ago and someday perhaps. But
punishing a cell and the prisoners in it
only gives old bars a new coating—shrunk
to a cynical husk, spitting out teeth and discourse,
you would throw back your head and think, thank God it's
    doomsday
and be stripped of sun forever. Come back,
then, tenderly, to your old home; looking around
at the hungry and the hobbling, always be ready to speak,
and when they make ribald comments about the curious gleam
in your eye, gather them up and begin:
partners in darkness, friends, I have seen such wonders.